I0652546

Ghoulish Thoughts Volume 3

By Mary Ann Streblow

This book is printed by Lulu.com for **Multi-Dimensions Press.** If there are any questions or comments about this book, please write to:

Multi-Dimensions Press
3101 North 67th Avenue
Omaha, NE 68104-3522
U.S.A.

ISBN # 978-0-6152-4543-0

Ghoulish Thoughts
Volume 3

By

Mary Ann Streblow

Dedication

This book is dedicated to Carol Elek and Sherri Kay Dobek. We are all sisters in search of answers from other realms.

Special thanks to Shari Reynolds for scanning the art work and typing this manuscript.

I also wish to thank the Omaha Libraries for their assistance.

Table of Contents for Stories

Table of Contents for Stories – Continued

Table of Contents for Poems

Table of Contents for Poems - Continued

Sh-h-h-! Some of the stories and poems are enough to wake the dead!

New Orleans Survives [Non-Fiction]

By Mary Streblow 2/5/07

New Orleans has survived

the hurricanes and the tides.

The neighboring towns are

rebuilding, as are corporate czars.

But where is FEMA?

Did they send money to Iwo Jima?

Much is promised, but little delivered.

What reaches the people are but slivers.

Fiery Touch

By Mary Streblow 2/5/07

Fire burns and purifies

while mankind hides behind lies.

Sadly, man will use fire

against man when flares his ire.

The flicker of the candle

looks so harmless to handle.

But from a tiny flame grows

the mega fires of old.

Mary Streblow ©2007

Nature's Autumn

By Mary Streblow 2/11/07

She dabbled in paint,

coloring the world.

Leaves of red and gold

sprinkled with some green.

Winds carried them off

from various trees.

They decorated the

landscape down below.

Society's Monsters

By Mary Streblow 4/18/07

It is said that

Society creates its own monsters.

That is often true.

Although Society created them,

it's the monsters that must

decide their actions.

The monsters can serve

good or evil.

They are in control.

Virginia Tech (Non-Fiction)

By Mary Streblow 4/18/07

The sound of gunfire
echoed in the halls.

Bullet fragments
tore apart the walls.

A madman killed
students and teachers.

His twisted soul
needed a preacher.

This sorrowful tale
happened on a Monday.

The date was April 16, 2007.
Cho had nothing to say.

Instead, he let the guns
speak their horrible sound.

He trapped his victims,
the doors were chain bound.

Where the Soul Lives

By Mary Streblow 2/5/07

Is the beating heart
the seat of one's soul?
The ancient ones thought
that this was the case.

Egyptian myth said that
a person's heart would be weighed.
No, not the actual weight,
but the weight of good deeds.

This would allow them
passage into a better life.
If they failed this test, they
would be sent to the nether world.

Mary Streblow
©2007

<u>Weeping Willow</u>
By Mary Streblow

Mad scientist, Dr. Vorkoff, decided to try some of his elixir on trees in a nearby forest. His goal was to have plants become intelligent and more mobile. That way they could defend themselves against pests and the weather.

When he returned to the woods, he found the weeping willow sad and crying. He patted it gently and asked, "What's wrong?"

The willow didn't have the gift of speech, only sound. So she pointed to the manly, black walnut with a limber branch. She wrote in the dirt with another branch:

He doesn't notice me at all!

Dr. Vorkoff shook his head. He thought, 'who would have known that plants could have crushes?'

Bitter Traveler
By Mary Streblow
10/04/07

He came out of no where,
he was just a puff of smoke.
Soon the smoke solidified,
becoming a vampire!
"Pull over!" he demanded.
"I want to drink your hot blood!"
I gripped the steering wheel
even tighter than before.
The gas pedal was down
to the floor of the old car.
"Never!" I shouted to
him before I turned sharply.
The right doors of my Nash
flew opened, sending him out.
The vampire tumbled to
the ground, shaking his fist.
"Have respect for your elders!"
he cried out in anger.
On the next turn left the
doors closed on my Nash Rambler.
'The vampire should have known
it wasn't safe to hitchhike.'
I smiled at the thought.
The car blinked its headlights.

Greensburg, Kansas (Non-Fiction)

By Mary Streblow 5/18/07

Hear the roar of the F-5 tornado,

Nature's angry ambassador.

It destroyed the town of

Greensburg, Kansas.

Its winds over 200 mph.

Its girth over a mile wide.

It was a miracle that people survived.

Nature's ambassador claimed over

eight lives on May 4, 2007.

It injured many more,

and made all homeless.

But the community refused

to surrender and began to

rebuild Greensburg again.

© 2007
mary Streblow

The Final Croak
By Mary Streblow
7/16/07

The frogs are vanishing,
so are the toads.
People are ignoring
this, building roads.

The newts are fewer,
and the salamanders too.
People want bright cities,
cheaper products, and new zoos.

All around lakes and ponds,
there is a growing silence.
Fewer animals live,
fighting a different violence.

Pollution and loss of
habitat, made nature broke.
People turned deaf ears,
not hearing the frog's final croak.

mary Streblow
(c) 2004

Dracula's Castle
By Mary Streblow
7/16/07

It had been taken from the Dracula family during the communists' reign. Then the castle was returned to the family and put up for sale in the year 2007.

Standing in the dark, Dracula wistfully looked at what was once his home. His pale face twisted with sadness.

"Who would believe that my castle is now up for sale?" Dracula asked his servant. "They want thirty-five million for it."

"But Master," said the sympathetic servant, "You've saved riches down from the ages. Couldn't they be used to pay for the castle?"

"No, for I have had to pay for many expenses over the years. I've not much to sell, not even stocks due to past markets."

The servant had let the information soak into his brain before he spoke. "Master, even though you do not pay me money, you provide room and board for me. Would it be better for you if I look elsewhere for employment?"

<u>Dracula's Castle - CONTINUED</u>

"No. For I will have need of you. Come, and we will return to our cottage. We will dine on fresh rabbit."

* Castle Dracula really did go up for sale for 35 million, in 2007. The communists had taken it and now the family has it back.

mary Streblow ©2007

Good or Bad?
By Mary Streblow [Non-Fiction]
7/16/07

There have been many reports of Gray aliens taking people aboard their ships. There they use various medical instruments to take samples, measurements, and sometimes afflict horrible procedures.

There have been reports of Gray aliens visiting humans to teach them. Teach them about peace and the return to nature.

Many people would like to believe that aliens don't exist at all. That way they wouldn't need to worry if Grays are good or bad. However, there has been too many reports, worldwide, to dismiss their existence.

It is my belief that both groups are right. Like humans, I believe there are good Grays and bad Grays. I do not believe their whole race is one or the other. Therefore we should be cautious with our encounters. Judge each Gray on their own actions.

Guns, Ammo and Land
By Mary Streblow
7/16/07

For years people have tried
to take guns away from the public.
"Guns kill people!" they cried.
When the truth is people kill people.

Our forefathers gave us rights
to bear arms for protection.
Countries that thought guns were blights
took away their citizens' freedoms.

This did not stop the killings.
Criminals still used guns.
Coffins were still in billings,
people continued to die.

Individuals need to keep
the right to defend themselves.
Governments hope their people sleep
so they can slip in new rules and laws.

If they can't take away the guns,
then they will take away the bullets.
Few shells for the daughters or sons,
most rounds are reserved for the government.

This is what the government plans
as they strive to regulate ammo.
Leaders want to make private lands
into public domain and high tolls.

© 2007
mary Streblow

On-Line
By Mary Streblow 5/18/07

Listen to the news!
What do you hear?
For more details,
go on-line.

Want to hear the Blues?
Or write to someone dear?
You won't fail
if you go on-line.

But there are those who
have no computer to use.
So they cannot
go on-line.

They must make do,
lacking money to pay dues.
Left behind, they
can't go on-line.

Long Distance
By Mary Streblow
6/22/07

Beretta Hill passed away in her sleep one May morning. She was 89, dark gray hair, and tall.

Among the mourners was a four-year-old-girl named Marreda. Like the adults, she was dressed in black, wearing black shoes. Unlike the adults, she felt confused.

"Where's Grandma?" Marreda asked as they sat on benches in the funeral home.

"She has been returned to ashes," Marreda's mother replied. "She is in the urn by the minister."

"The jar?"

"Yes."

Marreda puzzled over this information. She knew what ashes were, but also knew her grandmother was a tall woman. She couldn't figure out how she fit could into the jar. "Shouldn't we let Grandma out of the jar?"

Marreda's mother patted her hand and smiled. "No dear, Grandma is fine."

Long Distance (Continued)

Marreda stayed quiet the rest of the service. After the sermon, the people gave their sympathies and left the family at the funeral home. They had planned to have the urn buried during a private ceremony.

Before the father picked up the urn, Marreda tugged on his jacket. "Daddy, won't Grandma be lonely?"

"No, she is sleeping. When she's awake, she's with God."

"I think Grandma will be lonely if she can't call us. Can't you please put her phone with her?"

The father and mother exchanged glances. Then the father left, went to his car, and returned with his mother's cell phone. He had removed the batteries while at the car, not seeing a need to bury them with the phone.

"Alright, Marreda, this is Grandma's phone," the father said. He had the director open the urn, then seal it back up after he put in the phone. They buried the urn at Peaceful Valley Cemetary.

Two weeks went by before they started to get odd phone calls. The caller ID showed it was Marreda's grandmother calling them. The father and mother were perplexed, but their daughter was thrilled.

"Oh Grandma! I miss you!" Marreda gushed on the phone. She had reached it before her parents this time.

Long Distance (Continued)

"Marreda, give me the phone dear," her mother requested, frightened of what may be said by the person on the other end.

"No, Mommy. Grandma wants to talk to Daddy."

Marreda's father reluctantly took the phone. He said, "Hello?" His face turned white while he handed the phone back to his girl.

"What's wrong?" his wife asked. "Why did you give Marreda back the phone?"

"Mom just gave me hell for taking out the batteries of her cell phone. She said she would have called sooner if she would have had the batteries. Then Mom said to give Marreda the phone."

Beloved
Grandmother
Beretta Hill

Mary
Streblow © 2007

Zombie Dancer
By Mary Streblow
10/19/07

She danced gracefully.
Her movements were précised.
Her jade eyes were wide.
They were as empty as clear ice.

A spell had been placed
so she'd see no wrong.
If the controller wished,
he could have her sing a song.

He called her his beautiful,
obedient, zombie dancer.
She could not refuse his will
his power was like a cancer.

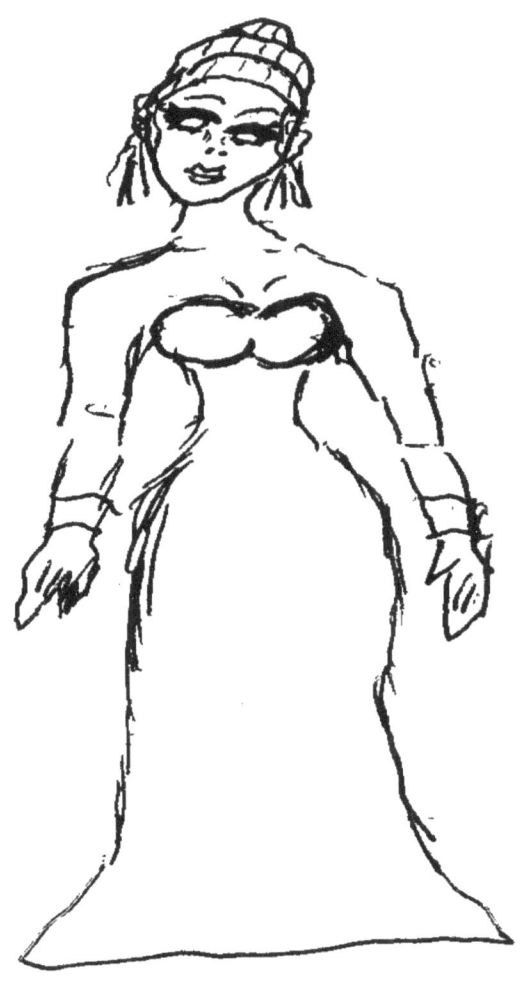

Fish Feed
By Mary Streblow
10/19/07

Another body thrown

into the wood chipper.

The parts flew into

the River Tripper.

All the river creatures

knew of the feed.

They flocked there,

waiting for the next deed.

Sometimes fisherman

found this secluded spot.

They'd pull out many fish,

not knowing the flesh that rot.

Peace on Earth
By Mary Streblow

An older woman went to a curio shop and saw that there was a monkey's paw for sale. She walked past it several times before picking it up.

"No, it can't be," she murmured to herself. Ada remembered reading the story of the monkey's paw as a child and how it gave three wishes. Unfortunately, the wishes carried terrible consequences.

Peace on Earth – Continued

Ada examined the paw closely. "It looks real enough."

"Oh, but it is," assured the shopkeeper. "But beware of what you wish for, for you may not get the wish how you thought it would come."

"So you're saying this is the monkey's paw? The same one from the story?" Ada stared at the man. His serious expression made her burst out with laughter. "Brother! You've just sold this monkey's paw!"

He murmured as he rang up the sale, "it wouldn't be the first time."

Ada took it home, turned on the TV, and listened to the news. There were wars in many parts of the world, as well as crimes. Ada took the paw out of the sack and held it with both hands. She said, "I wish for peace on earth!"

She vanished and appeared in a cemetery that stretched for miles. The last burial date she read as 2050.

"No-o-o!" Ada screamed. "I want to see life!"

To Ada's horror, hands began to burst through the graves, rotting corpses began to crawl out and head for her.

Ada screamed, "I want everything back as it was before I had made any wishes!"

Fortunately for Ada, she appeared back home. Ada ran back to the curio shop and returned the monkey's paw to the shop keeper.

The Monkey's Paw was written by William Wymark Jacobs

Night Wraith
By Mary Streblow
10/19/07

She comes out her grave every night,
hungry to feed on those that aren't right.

Her fangs drain their energy,
causing them to lose synergy.

Her claws tear into their flesh,
pouring warm blood through their mesh.

The Night Wraith's body is like a smoke.
Their cries of agony comes out in chokes.

Do not commit crimes, for you'll never know,
when will the Night Wraith reaps you as you sow.

Closet Ghost
By Mary Streblow

"The ghost in the closet is crying again,"

complained Dr. Vorkoff.

"How do you know it's a ghost?"

asked the nurse.

"Because it's crying BOO-who,"

Dr. Vorkoff replied.

"I recommend plenty of exercise," Dr. Vorkoff told his werewolf patient.

"Can I go running?" asked the werewolf.

"Yes, but avoid the Northwest Woods. After I gave some of the trees my elixir, the walnut trees have been pelting squirrels with nuts! Apparently, they don't feel appreciated."

If a witch married a werewolf, what would they have?

A wolf with a bad hair day. Or, a witch that howls at the moon.

<u>Lightning Gremlin</u>
By Mary Streblow
10/19/07

Who knew that in the sky,
a gremlin on lightning
would ride by?

From plane to plane he'd hop,
causing malfunctions at
every stop.

Electrical problems
here, lose nuts and bolts there.
Mad goblins!

Hold your seat tight flying!
One never knows what he
is prying!

<u>Find Me</u>
By Mary Streblow

I'm lost.
Please find me.
I'm scared.
Please find me.

Can you hear me?
Do you see me?
Can't you find me?
Am I invisible?

Worst of all,
you have seen me.
You have touched me.
You even heard my sounds.

My mind is trapped,
while my body lays limp.
I want to scream,
so you'd know I'm here.

Find Me

I can't do anything
except wait.
I might recover,
or I may not.

Hearts and Roses
By Mary Streblow

Dr. Vorkoff sat in the Café, barely touching his coffee. The waitress, who resembled a black panther due to her fur and tail, quietly stepped next to him. Eventually, she decided to break the silence.

"Dr. Vorkoff? Is there anything wrong with the coffee? Dr. Vorkoff?" Pur-fah asked.

"Huh?" he turned his head as if seeing her for the first time. "Coffee? Yah, it's fine."

"What's wrong?"

"Oh-h-h! It's that darn elixir! I wanted to improve the life of plants, not make it worse! I gave some to my bleeding hearts and to my white roses."

"So, what's wrong with that?" The waitress was puzzled.

"The bleeding hearts decided to bleed onto the white roses in a fit of jealousy. Then the white roses got depressed because they were stained. So they dropped their petals!" Dr. Vorkoff groaned.

The New Doctor
By Mary Streblow

Dr. Vorkoff frowned when he saw the new doctor in town. She stood only 5', 5", with silver hair and had to weigh about 300 pounds.

"You're kind of heavy to be a doctor," Dr. Vorkoff commented. "Maybe you should join a dieter's club?"

"You're kind of insane to be a doctor, from what I've heard." She quipped back as she squinted her blue eyes behind her glasses. "Maybe you should go to an asylum?"

"You've got a point there," Dr. Vorkoff pondered. "What's your name again?"

"Everyone calls me 'Dr. Foo,' because it's easier to say than my real name. It's been so long since I've been called anything else, I'd probably ignore it."

"Pleased to meet you," Dr. Vorkoff said politely. He wondered, 'so how much competition will she be? And, am I *really* pleased to meet her?'

Night Eyes
By Mary Streblow

Who's that lurking in the dark?

A goblin? Or a land shark?

No matter how we worry,

the fears creep in us early.

Anything can be in the dark.

Take care going into the park.

Ghost in the Closet
By Mary Streblow

Dr. Vorkoff heard the ghost in his closet coughing. The coughs were deep and rattling.

"Hey in there!" Dr. Vorkoff pounded on the door. "I am a doctor you know? I could cure you!"

The mirror on the wall became steamed up.   Then a message appeared. It read:

You're Not On My HMO.

Question: If a ghost and a skeleton could have children together, what might they have?

Answer: Skeletons with too much air in their bones, or ghosts with sheets too heavy with calcium.

The Storyteller and the Leprechaun
By Mary Streblow

Once there was a teacher of young children, named Jeanne Kuhn. To keep them entertained, she would tell stories about leprechauns, and would incorporate the youngsters' names into the plots as well.

What Jeanne didn't know was that the leprechauns loved listening to her stories too. They would hide in bushes by the opened windows, or hide behind the coats in the coat room.

All of this happened thirty-five years ago. The once spry teacher had grown older, her health failing. Instead of walking, she had to rely on a wheelchair, but her mind was still sharp. Jeanne still remembered the stories that she told the children.

"Hello, Jeanne Kuhn," a leprechaun stepped out of the shadows. "It's been a long time."

"A leprechaun!" Jeanne exclaimed. "I knew you were real! I just knew it!"

"Aye, we're real," he smiled. His red hair and whiskers were the color of rusty nails. "I missed hearing your leprechaun stories, and I was hoping you'd do me the honor of telling me some?"

The Storyteller and the Leprechaun - Continued

"Well," Jeanne pondered as she thought it over, "it's been a long time. Why don't you get a little closer so I don't have to talk so loudly?"

The leprechaun got closer. "Is this better?"

"Yes," Jeanne agreed. Then she began to spin various tales she had told the children years ago. At the end of her second story, she cleared her throat. "What is your name?"

"Michael Patrick O'Shaun, but everyone calls me Mike," the leprechaun replied.

"Well as you can tell, my voice isn't what it used to be." Jeanne cleared her throat again. "Why don't you come closer? Then I won't have to talk so loud."

So Mike got closer, close enough for Jeanne to touch him, but not to grab him. Just as Jeanne leaned forward to begin the next tale, she snatched his green hat with a clover on it!

"See here, Jeanne Kuhn! Gim-me back my hat!" The leprechaun tried to grab it back, but she held it too high for him to reach.

The Storyteller and the Leprechaun - Continued

"Not until you give me three wishes!" Jeanne smiled.

"What? Do you believe your own stories now? Do you think by grabbing my hat you've forced me to do your bidding?"

Jeanne shrugged, "It's worth a try. Besides, I've not much to lose."

"Aye," the leprechaun agreed, recalling her illness. "What can I do for you? Mind you, you've no power over me, it's just that it's my favorite hat. Besides, you've been telling nice stories about leprechauns for years, so maybe I can return the favor to you?"

"Make me well again," Jeanne requested.

"Oh-h-h lassie, I would if I could, but that's up to the Good LORD. For only HE has the power to do that."

Jeanne nodded sadly and returned the hat to Mike. "As you said, it was worth a try."

The Storyteller and the Leprechaun - Continued

Mike took the hat and blinked in surprise. "Aren't you going to ask for a pot of gold?"

"No, it'll be more trouble than it's worth. The government will want to know how and where I got the money from and they'd take away my benefits. Then they might not grant the benefits again when the money is gone." Jeanne sighed.

"You've a point there," Mike sighed after her. "Maybe there's a small wish or two that I can grant?"

Suddenly Jeanne's face lit up. "I want a warm shawl with pockets, a hat and matching gloves!"

"Done!" Mike provided the garments and sat them on her dresser.

"I want warm, non-skid slippers and a new, warm blanket."

"Done!" Mike set the items on her bed. "Anything else?"

Jeanne pondered. "I've been having problems with the phone company lying to me. Can you do anything for that?"

The Storyteller and the Leprechaun - Continued

Mike smiled a wicked smile. "Oh-h-h, lassie, I've just the thing!"

So the leprechaun cast a spell on the employees at the phone company. For every time they knowingly told a lie, their undergarments tighten. Some lied so much, that their voices hit new high octaves.

*Jeanne Kuhn is a real person and gave permission to use her name and lives in Omaha, Nebraska. Jeanne had taught preschool children and was a story teller of leprechaun tales which she created daily.

Mary Had A Little Roach
By Mary Streblow

Mary had a little roach,
its shell was brown, and a glow.
Everywhere Mary went,
the roach was sure to go.

It followed her from room
to room, waiting to consume.
Fast on its feet,
it stole its treat.

No matter how often it was killed,
the roach reappeared running still.
The insect drove Mary mad,
which made the roach glad.

For when Mary died one night,
the roach no longer took flight.
It crept inside her body dead,
keeping her company as it fed.

mary
Streblw
11/24/07

Donner
By Mary Streblow

A mother asked her child in December, "Can you name Santa's reindeers?"

The little girl nodded slightly, "Rudolf, Comet, Cupid, Blitzen, Dasher, Prancer, Vixen and Dancer."

The mother said, "Very good! But you're missing one. Do you know his name?"

"Donner, but they ate him at the Donner party." The girl confused the reindeer with the ill-fated pioneers crossing the mountains years ago.

Mary
Streblow 11/24/07

<u>Gentle Request (Wellington)</u>
By Mary Streblow

We had some wonderful times.

Our sparks flew like fireflies.

I'd like us to share our rhymes

and rhythms as our bodies tie.

The life and light in your eyes

fueled my spirit to great highs.

Sweet lady, I await thee.

Will you come forth and see me?

Nursing Home Syndrome
By Mary Streblow

They take us in as if they run a puppy mill. Our bodies stuff the building full.

They cut the hours of their nursing staff so much that many don't get the care they need. But they still take in more!

Isn't it funny how people are trying to stop people from "hoarding" animals, because they can't care for them? Yet, no one stops to think that this is what's happening in many nursing homes today?

Nov 2007
Mary
Streblow

Herbicide
By Mary Streblow

There was a knock on Dr. Vorkoff's door. When he opened it, to his dismay, stood Dr. Foo. She held what was left of his snap dragons.

"What did you do?" Dr. Vorkoff cried as he cuddled the remains.

"I was tending to my peonies when these snap dragons attacked me!" Dr. Foo answered gruffly. "If you insist on giving your plants various elixirs, then you had better put leashes on them! Otherwise, there'll be more herbicides!"

Dr. Vorkoff watched her leave. Then buried his snap dragons.

11/20/07
Mary Streblow

When Reindeer Go on Strike
By Mary Streblow

Santa examined his team of flying reindeer. They were in great shape. They had practiced all year to do their amazing speeds, not to mention being able to stop on a dime. They also had practiced being sure-footed, regardless of the ice and snow conditions.

"This is the night before the big flight. I want us to do one more warm up."

Comet stood behind Rudolf. He turned his head towards Santa. "No."

"What?" Santa bellowed. The jolly elf was no longer smiling and was shocked at the calm defiance. "What did you say?"

"No," Comet repeated firmly. "We're on strike."

When Reindeer Go on Strike - Continued

Rudolf did not turn around from his lead position. He stood like a lawn statue, not even moving his ears or eyes.

"You're on strike?" Santa repeated. "Why? Haven't I provided the best room and board for you? The finest feed? The freshest water? Why are you going on strike?"

This time Blitzen swung his head in Santa's direction. "Every year it's the same thing. We practice and practice until we're sick of practicing. Then we have to make the flight all over the world in a matter of hours without flaw."

"But that's what we do!" Santa held up his hands in jester of the world. "We deliver gifts all over the world in one night!"

When Reindeer Go on Strike - Continued

"No, that's what YOU do," snorted Cupid. "WE pull the sleigh. Other than the 'reindeer,' most people don't know our names! In fact, if it wasn't for that stupid song about Rudolf, no one would know our names!"

"But the poem, *The Night Before Christmas -,*" Santa didn't get to finish his statement.

"Was a long time ago," groaned Vixen. "Even the song about Rudolf is old, but it's catchy. We need new publicity."

"It- it's impossible to do that this year." Santa blinked his blue eyes while stroking his beard flat. "I can do it for next year."

When Reindeer Go on Strike - Continued

"No," Comet repeated firmly again. "We're not moving. Maybe if people don't get their gifts this year, they'll remember our names. It seems like they only remember the names of those that did bad."

"I can't believe this! I can't believe this!" Santa muttered as he stomped off.

Santa went inside the palace and sat down on his thrown. He propped his head with a fist, while resting his elbow on the chair's arm. "What can I do?"

To his surprise, a tall, Gray alien appeared before him. He bowed from the waist down in show of respect. His thin mouth didn't move as he spoke.

When Reindeer Go on Strike - Continued

"Dear Santa, it is part of my job to observe events on Earth. It would make me very happy to help you," said Lux-Zor.

"Help me? How?" Santa leaned forward eagerly.

"For just this year, your sleigh will be pulled by five, small, flying saucers. After that, you will have to work on the labor relations with your reindeer," said the Gray.

"Done!" Santa shook Lux-Zor's three-fingered hand.

Unknown to most humans, Christmas was saved by beings from another world. The reindeer became scared that their jobs would be outsourced. The strike ended.

Mary Streblow
Nov 2007

The Night of Halloween
By Mary Streblow

T'was the night of Halloween,

and all through the house,

the ghosts were stirring,

some even groused.

Pumpkins were carved

into jack-o-lanterns with care,

in hopes of creating a

spooky nightmare.

Haunting laughters

echoed through the halls,

while all matter of creatures

danced at the balls.

The thinnest veil began to

grow heavy at 4 AM,

so all candles were blown out

until Halloween came again.

mary
streblow
12/12/07

Stolen Copper (Non-Fiction)
By Mary Streblow

Thieves stole the copper from the Coppers' Training Center.   It was under construction, with the National Guard Center nearby. It seemed even the police weren't safe from robbers. This happened December 12, 2007 in Omaha, Nebraska.

12/12/07

mary
Streblow

Snow Angel
By Mary Streblow

The rabbit sat in the snow with her young son. They stared at the snow angel on the ground.

"Mama," said the son. "What matter of animal makes this mark?"

"Humans," she replied.

"Why? What does it symbolize?" The young rabbit hopped closer to the snow angel and examined it.

"Youth," the mother rabbit replied. "For I have only seen their cubs do this. They usually laugh as they do their markings. As they grow older, they stop marking the snow and laugh less often."

The Santa Gray
By Mary Streblow

No one had meant for it to happen, but there he was, lying in pain. His famous "Ho! Ho! Ho!" was replaced by "Oh! Oh! Oh!" He couldn't move his left leg without tripling the agony of just staying still.

Elves with a stretcher rushed to Santa's side. Like powerful ants, they gently hoisted their leader on the gurney and took him to the hospital wing of their empire.

"What was he thinking?" complained Tony, the head elf. "He's too old to rough house with reindeer or elves!"

Mrs. Claus had been pacing nearby. She was fretful both for her husband and because Christmas was only a week away.

"Oh, you know Papa," Mrs. Claus called her husband that, for he was like a father to the elves. "He's a kid at heart. He always will be."

Tony glanced at her and nodded. He was thinking this couldn't have happened at a worse time. As the top elf, he would have to decide how to proceed if Santa couldn't perform his duties.

The Santa Gray - Continued

The doctor came out with a grim expression. "Santa broke his left leg in two places and put a hairline fracture in his left arm when he tried to break his fall. There's no way he will be able to deliver gifts this year."

"O-o-h, no!" Mrs. Claus put a hand to her mouth. She knew Santa would be devastated if the presents weren't delivered.

"He wants to talk to both of you," the doctor continued. "Be sure not to encourage him on being able to make the trip. He must face his limitations realistically."

Tony entered the room, holding his pointed hat in his hand. Mrs. Claus followed behind the top elf, looking like a giant in comparison.

Santa knew things weren't good by their sober expressions. Tony rarely took his hat off except for funerals and other sad occasions. Santa wondered briefly, 'When did Tony's hair start turning gray?' Santa's thoughts got lost on the silver strands among the black hair.

The Santa Gray - Continued

"Santa?" Tony tried to draw the big man's attention. "Santa? You do realize you can't fly this year, don't you? The doctor did talk to you about it, right?"

Mrs. Claus silently fluffed the old man's pillows and got fresh ice for his water pitcher. She hung up Santa's jacket in the closet, and placed his boots in there as well.

"I'll clean your boots later, Papa," Mrs. Claus announced. "Papa? Are you listening to Tony? You can't make the flight this year."

"Hum? Yes, yes, I know that!" Santa waved his hand.

"What do you want us to do?" Tony asked.

"I have an idea," grinned Santa. "Remember how we stopped the Reindeer Strike of 2006?"

Tony frowned slightly. "We had some folks from another world pull the sleigh with their flying saucers. But how is that going to help us now? The reindeer are willing, but there's no driver."

The Santa Gray - Continued

"Lux-Zor, that Gray that came to help us," Santa pondered, "maybe he can drive the sleigh?"

"What?" Tony stared at the big man in disbelief. "That's not something a person learns to do overnight! I mean, Bongo has practiced off and on for five years, and I'm not sure if he's ready for the big flight!"

Cory "Bongo" Mitts loved playing the bongos on his down time. He would get lost in the beat of the mini-drums as his blond, wavy locks bounced.

Tony walked three steps agitated, back and forth in front of Santa. He pointed out, "I don't know how the reindeer will react to Lux-Zor! First of all, he was the one that killed their strike! Second of all, you know how they feel about 'strangers' taking the reigns."

Santa shook his head. "When the strike ended, both sides promised not to hold it against the other. This is a different situation all together. There's no choice but to have a different driver."

"Bongo ---."

The Santa Gray - Continued

"Bongo is nice, as well as dependable," Santa interrupted, "But he's too slow. He needs to work on his speed and confidence. Lux-Zor has had lots of practice working at high speeds."

"But we have no way to contact him!" Tony shouted with finality.

"Yes we do," Santa stated quietly as he retrieved a pager from his pant pocket. He pressed the button and Lux-Zor appeared by his bedside.

"Santa?" Lux-Zor questioned as he stared at the big man's leg in a cast.

"Lux-Zor, I need another tremendous favor from you. As you can see, I won't be able to fly my sleigh this Christmas. Could you take over this year? We'd appreciate it so much!"

Lux-Zor nodded. "I'll do it for you, Santa."

On Christmas Eve, 2007, the gifts were delivered without a hitch. Those that managed to sneak a peak at Santa, worried that he was too thin.

The Santa Gray - Continued

Others didn't see rosy cheeks, but silver-gray. Only one little girl saw Lux-Zor as the Gray that he was. Lux-Zor had dressed in a similar red and white suit, with the pointed hat and black boots to try to fool people at a distance.

However, Connie saw his huge black eyes and three fingered hands while he placed presents under the tree. Lux-Zor turned and smiled slightly as he hoisted the sack back over his shoulder.

"Are you Santa?" Connie asked.

"No, my sweet child, I am a friend. Santa isn't feeling well, so I'm helping him out."

"Oh." Her brown eyes got big as she comprehended his words. "Please take my gift back and give it to Santa. I don't have anything else to give him and I want him to get well."

"Are you sure?"

"Yes."

The Santa Gray - Continued

Lux-Zor picked up a gift in red foil with a green bow. He returned it to his bag, then went up the chimney like old St. Nick.

It wasn't until after he delivered all the other gifts that he returned to Santa. He gave the big man the present as promised.

Lux-Zor said, "Connie wanted you to have her Christmas present in hopes it would make you feel better."

Santa took it and wept. He thought proudly, 'The Christmas Spirit is alive and well . . .'

© 2007
mary
Streblow

Flowers, Not Candy
By Mary Streblow

While on Earth, Lux-Zor, the Gray alien, learned about Valentine's Day. He thought, 'anyone can *buy* candy. I'll *make* some candy instead.'

While in the process of mixing ingredients he discovered he did not have enough sugar. Lux-Zor pondered, 'surely Dr. Vorkoff has sugar at his house. I'll ask him.'

Lux-Zor almost reached Dr. Vorkoff's door when he slipped on an oily substance on the sidewalk. He fell into the flower bed with a scream. The flowers were also covered with the goo, so some of their petals and leaves stuck to him.

"Oh my gosh!" Dr. Vorkoff ran out his front door. "I am so sorry!"

The doctor helped Lux-Zor up. He plucked the leaves and most of the petals off the Gray alien.

"I am so sorry!" Dr. Vorkoff said again. "I wasn't expecting company, or I would have been more careful with my elixir."

"Elixir? What sort of elixir?" Lux-Zor became alarmed.

"Oh, don't worry! It's nothing harmful, I assure you."

"What sort of elixir?" Lux-Zor asked more firmly.

"It makes flowers grow bigger. It's nothing to worry about. I – I wanted to give a friend of mine a nice surprise of flowers is all."

"OK," Lux-Zor sighed. "It sounds harmless enough."

Flowers, Not Candy - Continued

Neither had paid attention to the small petals around Lux-Zor's throat. They were so tiny, that they weren't even an eight of an inch in length.

"I came here for two cups of sugar," Lux-Zor explained to Dr. Vorkoff. "May I have it for making candy?"

"Well, I'm sure I have a cup of sugar, but I don't think I have two cups. You might have to use sweetener for the rest."

"Oh!" Lux-Zor pondered. "I wonder how well that'll work?"

"It should work," Dr. Vorkoff said with confidence. "Stay here and I'll get the sugar. I don't want you to have another accident by going inside."

In a couple of minutes, Dr. Vorkoff returned. He handed Lux-Zor a plastic container. "There's a cup and a half of sugar in there. Sorry, that's all I had."

"Thanks, doctor!" Lux-Zor took it back to his rented house and finished making the candy. He decided to add more chocolate chips since he had less sugar. It didn't turn out too bad, but wasn't as smooth as he would have liked it.

Lux-Zor went to bed, wondering if he should get something else for his wife, Lei-Mar, for Valentine's Day. The next morning he was shocked by the large, yellow flower petals around his neck. He ran to Dr. Vorkoff's.

Dr. Vorkoff stumbled to his door and opened it. He awoke instantly upon seeing Lux-Zor. "Oh my!"

Flowers, Not Candy - Continued

"Look at this!" Lux-Zor demanded. "These petals are *attached* to me! I went to pull them and my skin wanted to go too!"

"Calm down! Calm down! You'll be happy to know the effects are only temporary." Dr. Vorkoff assured him. "It'll only last a day or two, then the pedals will fall off."

"You're sure?"

"Oh, yes! I had the same thing happen to me a month ago."

"OK," Lux-Zor sighed. "I think I can handle looking like a flower for a day or two."

Dr. Vorkoff watched the Gray alien leave. He murmured, "I just hope Grays are affected the same way as humans, or we're both in trouble!"

Lux-Zor decided to make the best of the situation. He made a hologram message for his wife as a gift.

"Hello, my little zorlock!" Lux-Zor said into the floating camera. "I send you my love and heart! I decided that I will be your flower for Valentine's Day. I wish I could be home with you, but I want you to know I always think about you."

Lux-Zor pressed a button on the camera, which was black, round, and the size of a baseball. It zoomed away to deliver its message.

When Lei-Mar saw the hologram, she smiled. She thought, 'Lux-Zor always finds a way to give me something special on Valentine's Day. I really love him for sharing that Earth holiday with me!'

Flowers, Not Candy
By Mary Streblow

Mary Streblow
1/8/08

Housebreaking
By Mary Streblow

"Oh!" Pur-fah moaned as she looked outside the *Haunted Café's* window. "It's raining! That'll mean my fur will get wet! And you know how us cats love water!"

Dr. Vorkoff looked up from his steaming cup of coffee. He chewed his first bite of his bagel, ham and cheese sandwich, then swallowed. "Raining, huh? Well, I might be able to help in the future. But I'm afraid I can't do anything about it tonight."

"Oh well," Pur-fah shrugged. "I guess it won't kill me to get wet. I've been drenched before and survived."

Dr. Vorkoff laid five dollars on the table after finishing his sandwich and coffee. He told Pur-fah, "Keep the change. I heard the weather report this morning, they expect another storm tomorrow night. So hopefully I'll have a solution by then."

"Yah," remarked the cook unkindly, "it's called an umbrella."

Housebreaking - Continued

Pur-fah shot a glare at the cook, who looked like a mixture of a man and a raptor, such as a hawk or eagle. "Don't mind Manny, Doc. He was born a smart-aleck!"

Dr. Vorkoff nodded, then left. He thought, 'Isn't it bad enough that I have Dr. Foo's remarks to contend with, and now Manny's?'

The doctor worked through the night and put a mixture inside a rocket. Early in the morning, he fired it into the sky. The rocket reached a great height, then exploded into multi-colored sparks. It reminded him of the 4th of July.

'The particles will stay in the air and attach themselves to the clouds,' thought Dr. Vorkoff. 'Then we'll see how well my concoction works!'

By noon, the skies were heavy with clouds. Then it began to sprinkle.

Housebreaking - Continued

Dr. Vorkoff showed up at the *Haunted Café* fifteen minutes before ten-o-clock. Despite the heavy rain, he was dry.

"Doc! You did it! You did it without an umbrella!" Pur-fah shouted.

"OK, Dr. Vorkoff, how'd you do it?" Manny grumbled.

"Well, this is only temporary mind you, but I created a different form of my elixir. When it was just sprinkling outside, I tried to 'housebreak' the clouds."

"Housebreak the clouds? Don't that mean they have to be *alive*?" Pur-fah asked.

"Yah, yah," Dr. Vorkoff said hesitantly. "A little bit alive, just for tonight."

"Hump!" Manny grumbled, "this I've got to see!"

Dr. Vorkoff and Pur-fah stepped outside first. They walked into the parking lot, ten feet from the café's door. They remained dry, as did the rest of the parking lot.

Housebreaking - Continued

Manny came outside complaining to the clouds, "do you know how many times you wrecked the wax job on my car?"

Water poured on Manny while he looked up into the sky. He spat out the water that fell into his mouth.

"Like anything else, if you make the clouds nervous or upset, they will pee on you." Dr. Vorkoff stated.

The Gray Bunny
By Mary Streblow

"I quit!" yelled the woman in the rabbit suit. "The kids are little monsters! Get someone else to play the Easter bunny!"

The woman took off her suit and stormed off. Fortunately, she was wearing her regular clothes beneath the suit.

"What am I going to do?" wailed the church woman. "The children expect an Easter bunny and eggs! I can't fit into the suit! Besides I don't hop well anymore!!"

Lux-Zor, the Gray alien, stared at the pink rabbit suit on the ground. He shrugged, "I can fit into the suit."

"Oh bless you!" The church woman gave him a hug. "It'll mean so much to the children!"

Lux-Zor slipped the suit on and picked up the basket of plastic Easter eggs. The eggs were filled with candy and little toys. He hid the eggs on the edge of the flower garden, behind trees and ornamental grasses, as well as the empty fountain. Lux-Zor realized that the goal was to

The Gray Bunny – Continued

entertain the children and not make it impossible to find the eggs.

He said to the church woman, "all finished!"

"Excellent!" she beamed with joy. "Could you lead the hunt? That is, give the children the signal that it's time to look for the eggs?"

"Sure." Lux-Zor hopped over to a group of excited children.

"Ready?"

"Ready!" they screamed in unison.

"Go!"

The children poured forth, collecting eggs and putting them in their baskets. Lux-Zor and the church woman watched, both were happy things were going so well.

"I want to thank you again, Lux-Zor, for your help. Is there anything I can do for you?" asked the church woman.

The Gray Bunny – Continued

"Yes, I'm curious as to what kind of chickens lay the real Easter eggs? I've never seen eggs that were three or more bright colors before. I'd like to take some of the chickens to our zoo."

She held up an actual egg. "These are eggs that come from various chickens. They normally start out as white, and we use dyes to color them. They're not laid that way."

"Oh," Lux-Zor sighed in disappointment. "Once again make-up is applied to enhance something's features. Nothing is natural."

The Gray Bunny

By Mary Streblow

mary Streblow   1/8/08

Westroads [Non-Fiction]
By Mary Streblow

On December 5, 2007, people were shopping as usual at the Westroads Mall. It was Wednesday, after 1:00 pm, and people had their minds on Christmas gifts.

A young man named Robert "Robbie" Hawkins wanted to become famous. So in cold blood, he killed eight people with a rifle at Von Maur, before ending his own life.

Robert had the right name. For the first part, "Rob," is what he did when he stole those people's lives.

They said he had mental issues and people tried to help him. However, resources were either limited or Robert refused treatment. If he is to become famous, then let it be used to encourage Nebraska to help those with mental health problems. For Omaha no longer has Richard Young to treat patients.

<u>Westroads – Non-Fiction</u>

By Mary Streblow

Mary Streblow
1/8/08

Eviction
By Mary Streblow

The tenant ran over to his landlord and complained, "I have a huge roach problem!"

"OK, I'll take care of it," the landlord grumbled. He wondered how bad it really was, and how much poison he would need?

The landlord went to apartment marked "12" and opened the door. To his shock, a six-foot tall roach stood there; its antennae waving. Shaken, the landlord slammed the door shut and returned to his office. The tenant was still there.

"You don't have a *huge* roach problem! You have a GIANT roach problem! What do you want me to do about it?" The landlord trembled.

"I want you to serve an eviction notice!" stated the tenant firmly. "If he's not going to pay for his share of the rent, then out he goes!"

Eviction
By Mary Streblow

Birth of the Wee People

As the bubbling, green brew boiled over,

Drops of it spilled onto the white clover.

The plants began to move, lifting one root,

Then another; the roots turned into boots.

Legs sprang from the boots, growing inches long.

At one point the legs appeared, and there was song.

Where the legs merged, they formed strong ribs and trunk.

The flowers formed human heads that *thunk.*

The leaves rolled up tight and formed human arms.

From the arms grew hands; sleeves with cuffs had charms.

The beings had musical skills and sang.

They loved yellow gold to wear, *clink* or *bang.*

Their clothes were bright green, but gold made them mean.

Leprechauns were born, their minds very keen.

This poem originally appeared in Ghoulish Thoughts, Vol 1. Corrections have been made.

mary Streblow
© 2005

<u>Frozen Figure [Non-Fiction]</u>
By Mary Streblow

Pictures from the Mars rover showed a form that resembled a small human. The figure was in a sitting position with an arm stretched out.

Could this be the mummified remains of an ancient Martian? Or, maybe even the remains of an ancient Earthling brought there to be studied?

For now it is an unsolved mystery. Let us hope it will still be there when the first astronauts land on Mars.

<u>Melvin</u>
By Mary Streblow

Dr. Vorkoff stroked the red goatee on his chin as he stared at the 100-year-old patient. Melvin had came to him for a check up just a week ago. The man's organs were that of a 45-year-old man!

"I tell you, Doc, I have troubles being intimate with my wife. It just started two weeks ago." Melvin grumbled.

"Do you smoke?" asked Dr. Vorkoff.

"Two packs every day for 80 years."

"Do you drink?"

"Oh, I have either three beers a day, or two shots of whiskey. You know, I don't want to over do it," Melvin replied. "I've been drinking for 85 years."

"Have you done anything different lately? Or have you stopped doing something?" Dr. Vorkoff questioned in frustration. "Everything appears to be healthy!"

"Well, this is embarrassing," Melvin said after he pondered in thought. "I stopped seeing my mistress a month ago."

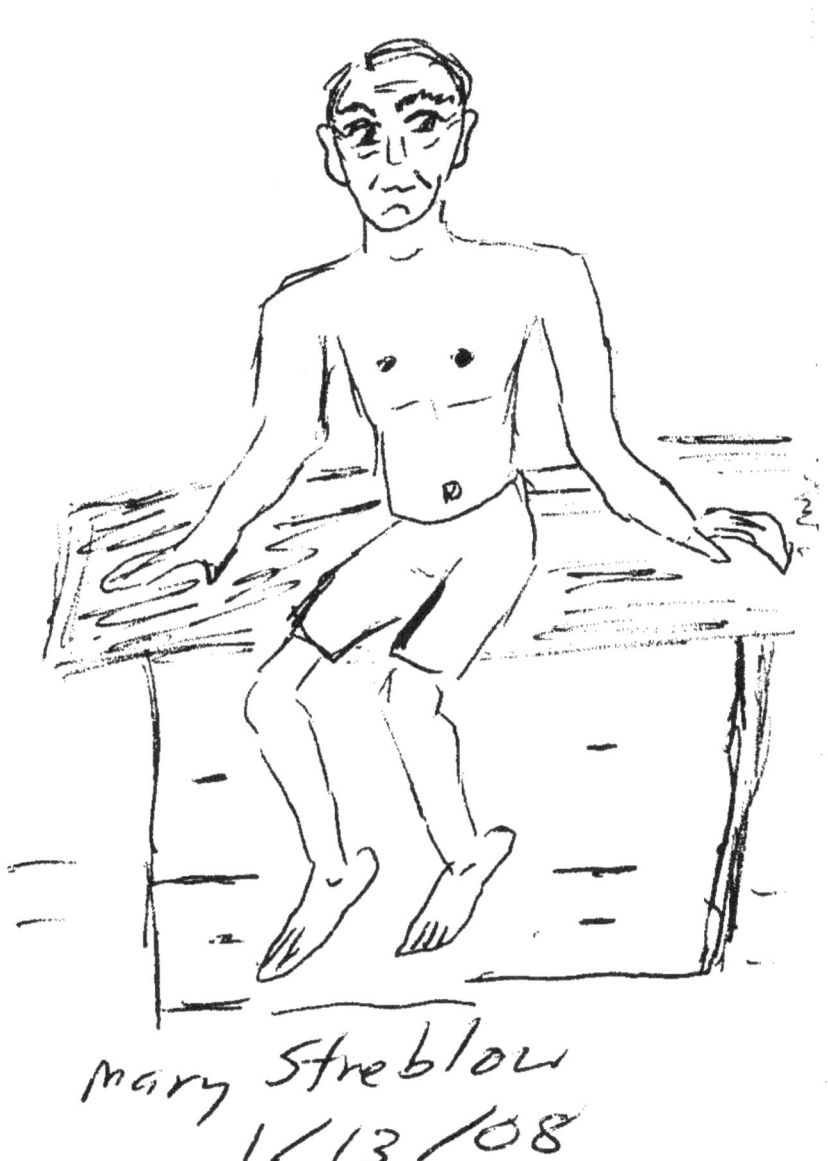

Skeleton at the Feast
By Mary Streblow

The wedding celebration was huge. Over two hundred people showed up. Drinks and food flowed freely. The festivities went on for twelve hours before the special guest arrived.

The high priestess, who had presided over the wedding, demanded silence. "Ladies and gentlemen, I give you Many Great Grandmother Ylitka!"

Two men carried in a chair on two poles. Sitting in the chair was the mummified remains of Grandmother Ylitka, draped in a blue robe. All except the high priestess bowed from the waist down in a great wall of silence. When they stood up straight, they resumed drinking, eating and dancing.

When it reached the thirteenth hour, all fell quiet and stood still. The priestess held up a goblet of wine in a toast. "To Many Great Grandmother Ylitka, the head of the family! May she always remind us that the road of life takes us to the path of death!"

Everyone drank deeply. For no one knew when they would travel death's road. On Timezonia, no one feared death, for it was just another part of life.

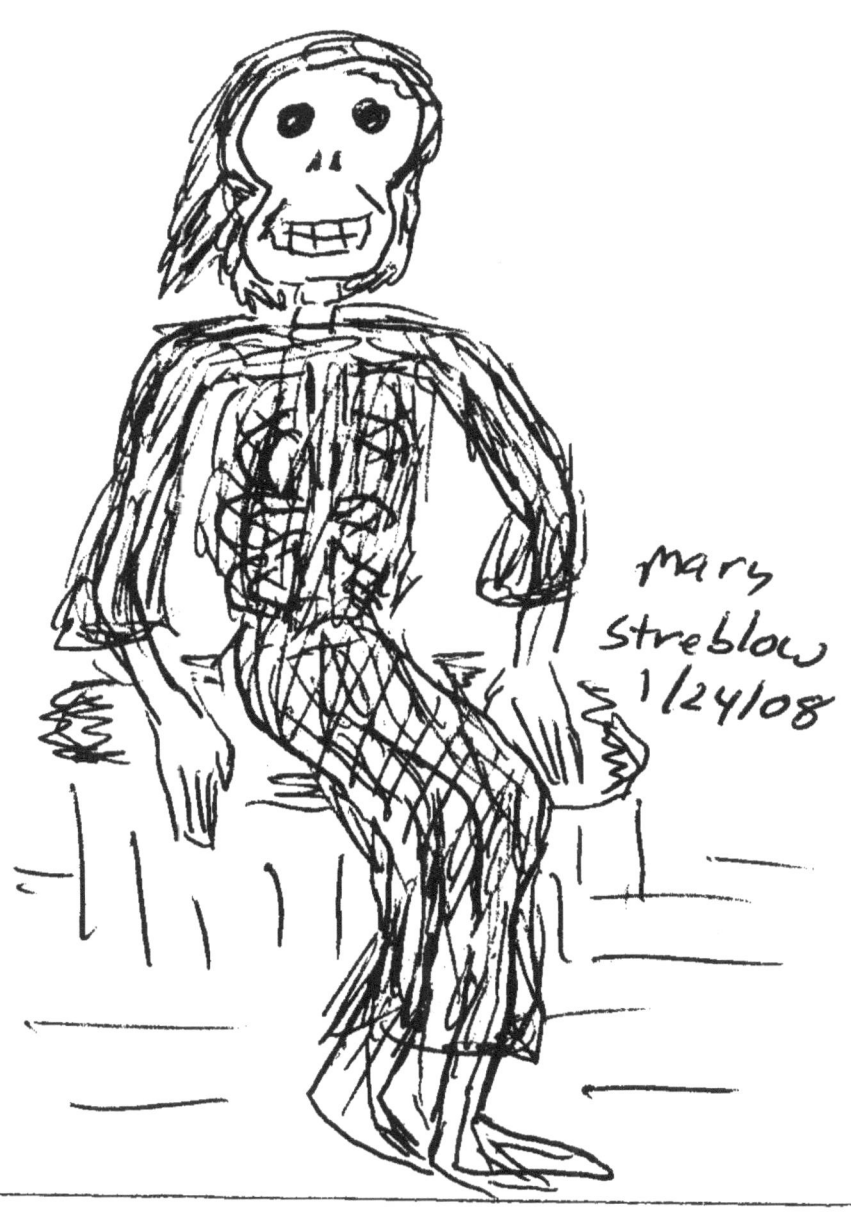

mary
Streblow
1/24/08

Tenants
By Mary Streblow

Pur-fah, the waitress at the *Haunted Café*, was writing in her journal while on break. She wasn't sure of the spelling of a certain word. She looked up and saw Dr. Foo drinking coffee and reading a book at another table.

Pur-fah timidly went over to the gray-haired doctor. "Excuse me, Dr. Foo?"

Dr. Foo looked up from her book, with a grim expression. She hated being disturbed when she was involved in anything. "Yes?"

"I – I'm sorry to bother you, but how do you spell 'tenant?' Is it t-e-n-d-a-n-t? Or, t-e-n-t-a-n-t?"

"Neither," replied Dr. Foo. "It is t-e-n-a-n-t. You can remember this by repeating: A tenant has the power of ten ants if he has the right judge."

"But it sounds like there should be a 't' or 'd' in the middle!"

Dr. Foo shrugged, "That's the wonderful thing about dialects and the English language."

mary Streblow
1/13/08

Music Man
By Mary Streblow

He banged a way,
not missing a note.
He played beautiful
music as he jolt.

The bony xylophone
pinged like the finest China.
Who would have thought
it once was Ryna?

Ryna had been a
good friend of Vide.
So in death, Ryna
stayed by his side.

They continued their
concert for years,
until Vide died.
The crowd shed tears.

Mary
Streblow
1/25/08

Chickens
By Mary Streblow

Three women dressed in British military garments walked down the dirt road. They were in search of fresh food for themselves and their fellow soldiers.

"I'm so hungry, I'm actually trying to come up with a recipe to improve the taste of dirt!" Pink Flame grumbled in her Australian accent.

"Oh-h-h!" Yellow Flame groaned. "I'm so hungry, that hot water is beginning to look like a banquet!"

Millie, the tall Mexican, did not understand what her companions were saying. She felt the rumbling in her stomach and said in Spanish, "If only we could find an abandoned truck with food in it! Or maybe it could rain and freeze on a duck's wings? That can happen in high altitudes!"

About two hundred feet behind them, Colonel Miny Time followed. She preferred to make sure no one would be able to sneak up on her associates. Despite of the distance, she was able to hear the conversation.

Chickens – Continued

"Hey!" Pink Flame, a medical officer and a major, stopped suddenly. One arm blocked her half sister, Yellow Flame, from going further. Her other arm prevented Millie from going further. "Do you see what I see?"

Both followed Pink Flame's gaze through a grove of trees. Barely visible was a farmer trying to gather up his chickens. His truck had hit a bump in the road, causing several crates to fall out and open.

The three women hurried over, startling the farmer. He was relieved to see their uniforms weren't German. He spoke in French, "Ladies, what are you doing out here? Do you not know its dangerous?"

Pink Flame understood some French, but spoke it poorly. Her face betrayed her hunger. She pointed to the chickens. "Food, please."

Chickens – Continued

Millie didn't understand French at all. If it wasn't for the few that could speak Spanish in the troop, she would be completely isolated.

Yellow Flame was able to speak it flawlessly. She told the farmer, "We are in search of food for our soldiers. Perhaps we can work out a deal? We can help you catch the chickens in trade."

First the farmer's face was serious, then slowly he had an amused smile. A chicken strutted by, pecking at some insects before moving on. "Yes! It sounds good! I will give you all the eggs that they lay for 24 hours if you catch them!"

Yellow Flame told the deal to Pink Flame in English. Then the pale communications officer asked her half sister, "What do you think? Everyone would really appreciate fresh eggs!"

Chickens – Continued

Pink Flame considered it carefully before replying, "Tell him that we want the eggs that are laid by the chickens still in the crates as well as those that we catch. Then we have a deal!"

Yellow Flame told him. He responded, "But of course! It's a deal!"

"It's a deal!" Yellow Flame repeated. Then she said in Spanish to Millie, "We'll be rewarded by the farmer if we help him catch the chickens!"

Millie nodded and the three of them spread out. The chickens were fast, and some evaded capture. Those that were gathered by the women fought back. The three suffered from scratches and sores from being pecked. Their hair had become disheveled and their clothes suffered some tears. They shoved the chickens back into the crates and latched them.

"OK, chickens!" Pink Flame rubbed her hands together in anticipation. "Start laying eggs!"

Chickens – Continued

"When do they usually lay their eggs?" Yellow Flame asked, "Will we have to wait long?"

Colonel Miny Time joined the group, carrying two chickens in each hand. The birds had been stunned, so did not protest being carried upside down by their legs. She queried, "Major, Captain, did you ask how many chickens were hens?"

"Huh?" Pink Flame turned towards Miny Time the same time Yellow Flame did.

Yellow Flame's face showed confusion and repeated in English, "How many are hens? All of them, right?"

Meanwhile the farmer tried to get the four chickens from Miny Time by grabbing the birds' thighs. She refused to release them to him. He began to swear in French at her stubbornness.

Yellow Flame became cross and asked him bluntly in French, "How many are hens?"

Chickens – Continued

The farmer stopped trying to get the chickens back. He pulled his hands away, studying the faces of the four women.   He saw accusation as well as hunger and determination.

"I – I just had a little joke!" the farmer held up his thumb and index finger to symbolize a small amount.

"How many are hens?" Yellow Flame asked firmly. "Tell the truth or face the consequences!"

"They – they're all roosters. It's just a little joke!" the farmer tried to reassure them again. "I needed your help to catch the birds. Surely you can understand that. After all, you are here to liberate France from Germany! You do not want the Germans to get the chickens, do you?"

"Very well," Miny Time replied in French. "Now we will play a little joke on you! We will keep these four chickens as payment!"

Chickens – Continued

"What? No! No! Give them back!" The farmer tried to reach for them. He had not heard Yellow Flame speak Spanish to Millie. She told Millie, the transportation officer, what was taking place, and that the farmer wanted to welsh on payment for assistance.

The farmer felt Millie's heavy hand on his left shoulder. She hissed in Spanish, "give us the chickens willingly or you will be missing teeth!"

The farmer saw the deadly glare in Millie's eyes. Even though he didn't understand Spanish, there was no confusion as to the meaning being unhealthy for him.

"Go! Take the chickens! We will call it even! Right?"

"Yes," Yellow Flame agreed. "I am glad you did not press the 'joke' any further. My friend would have removed your teeth if you did!"

Chickens – Continued

The farmer nodded. He did not doubt Millie's capability of doing so.

He waited until the women were far away before lamenting, "They are worse than Germans! They steal my chickens while wearing British uniforms! Then they claim they're here to liberate France!"

Unknown to the farmer, Colonel Miny Time had handed the fowl to the others with orders to get the food back to the company. She doubled back and heard the Frenchman's rantings.

In perfect imitation of two Germans talking loudly, Miny Time held a conversation with herself. As the voice of one male, German, private, she said, "Orders were to gather all food stores and take them back to camp!"

"What if there's resistance from the French?" Miny Time asked in a deeper German voice.

"Shoot them! It is them, or us!" Miny Time watched the farmer's reactions.

Chickens – Continued

He hurried to his truck and drove off. The farmer suddenly realized that four chickens weren't a bad price to pay to for fighting the Germans that occupied his country!

Miny Time returned to her camp. The soldiers, American and British, had already cleaned the fowl and were cooking them. To feed their company they made a chicken, vegetable soup. The meal was like a banquet to them.

Pink Flame had a sad expression on her face as she ate her soup. She muttered to Yellow Flame, "I still had my heart on fresh eggs. Why couldn't *one* of them have been a hen?"

To learn more about these characters,
please read *Tales In The Dark.*
www.trafford.com/robots/03-1343.html

Walk-About
By Mary Streblow

Two women trekked a steady pace in the wilderness. Both were dressed in khaki shirts and slacks. Both wore heavy hiking boots and wool socks; each carried a backpack and canteen. From there, the similarities ended.

Major Sapphire "Pink Flame" Flame stood five feet tall, mahogany skin, with natural henna red hair. The other woman was slightly taller, with skin of fresh whitewash, and hair of spun gold. Oddly, they were half sisters.

"You've been to England so many times, yet, this is my first time to the Australian interior," said Capt. Goldie "Yellow Flame" Flame. "Will we reach your home soon?"

Walk-About - Continued

"We're here!" Pink Flame grinned as she continued to walk. "*All* of this is home. Mom and I often went on *Walk-Abouts,* and treated those in need of medical help. We didn't care who wanted aid, we just gave it to them."

"*Went* on *Walk-Abouts*? I thought *Walk-About* was the name of a bed and breakfast!"

Pink Flame burst into laughter. "This isn't jolly old England! Naw! *Walk-About* is an activity. One collects one's thoughts, but in this case, Mom and I also provided medical services."

"It's just that - "

"Stop!" Pink Flame ordered. "Stay where you are!"

Yellow Flame froze; her breathing became cut in half.

Walk-About - Continued

Only her sapphire blue eyes darted about trying to locate the danger. Her eyes didn't spot the brown serpent that her half sister saw.

In a swift movement, Pink Flame grabbed the back of the neck of the snake with one hand. The other hand picked up the mid-section of the six-foot beast.

The reptile hissed angrily and would have bitten both if it had the opportunity to do so. Pink Flame kept a firm grip on the head, but the mid-section escaped her other hand.

"This here is a Taipan snake," Pink Flame stated calmly in her thick Australian accent. "They're highly poisonous. You'd be a goner if he'd bit you."

Walk-About - Continued

The snake flickered his tongue at the sisters. Its body began to coil up even though Pink Flame still held it by the neck.

Yellow Flame exhaled slowly. Her once frozen body began to shake. "You – you – you're going to – to kil – kill it, aren't you?"

"Naw, it's not the snake's fault he doesn't like blondes. I'll take it a safe distance before releasing it." Pink Flame grabbed the snake's mid-section with her free hand again.

"A safe distance? What – what about the – the next country?" Yellow Flame continued to quake as she realized how close to death she came. She watched her half sister vanish with the serpent, wishing Pink Flame would kill it instead of setting it free.

Walk-About - Continued

"I survived bloody World War II! I lived through various dangerous assignments in the Colonies! Then I'm to nearly be murdered by a reptile! Jove! Wouldn't that be a lovely thing on my tombstone!" Yellow Flame fumed.

Pink Flame swiftly reappeared by her half sister. She saw the fire in the blonde's eyes.

"When I said I wanted to visit your home, I suppose you intentionally led me to that snake!" Yellow Flame yelled. "You probably had it planted right there!"

A grin spread acrossed the mahogany chemist's face. "Naw! I'd never want to upset the Taipan that bad. . . , it's just not neighborly! Now if I'd wanted to get rid of ya, I'd just introduce you to the crocs. Them saltys have voracious appetites, and there'd be no body for me to get

Walk-About - Continued

rid of!" Pink Flame winked. "Let's travel one more mile before we make camp."

"Camp?" Yellow Flame asked as they resumed their pace. *"We have to camp outside?"*

"Yah, that's why we have the backpacks."

"What if another Taipan shows up?" Yellow Flame wrung her hands. "It might crawl into the tent with me!"

"Just don't snore," Pink Flame smirked. "They hate that."

"What about Funnel Spiders? I've heard they're deadly!"

"No worries! They're mainly on the East Coast. That's why they're called *Sydney* Funnel Spiders. Most of them can read maps so don't get lost and end up in other

Walk-About – Continued

areas."   Pink Flame joked slightly.   Then she became serious. "We've had our ups and downs, and often don't see eye-to-eye. . . , but I'm glad you came."

Yellow Flame smiled back at her half sister. "I think that's the nicest thing you've ever said to me."

"Well, don't repeat it, or I'll have to talk to my lawyer. I'll sue you for slander of character!" Pink Flame winked.

Yellow Flame gave her a bewildered look. "But your lawyer is my lawyer, too."

You can read more about these characters in Tales in the Dark.
www.trafford.com/robots/03-1343.html

Walk-About - Continued

Author Bio

Mary Ann Streblow is a resident of
Omaha, Nebraska.   In 1977, she graduated
from Benson High. In 1979, she graduated from
Nebraska College of Business.

Mary has been writing since the 4th grade.
Author Lester Dent, a.k.a. Kenneth Robeson,
was her main inspiration.

Ghoulish Thoughts
Volume 1

By Mary Ann Streblow

Ghoulish Thoughts, Volume 1, is a composition of poetry, jokes, riddles, short stories, and art. It is meant to both entertain and provoke thought. It is not for the squeamish, for there are many **dark** elements presented.

Some stories are comparable to the violence in the TV series *Night Stalker* and *X-Files.*

Available at: www.lulu.com/content/182140

GHOULISH THOUGHTS
VOLUME 2

By Mary Ann Streblow

This book contains short stories, poems, art, and a small amount of jokes/riddles. Some writings deal with true events. Due to the dark nature of several items, this should be considered for teenagers and up.

Available at: ww.lulu.com/content/540390

Gray Folks: Earth and Beyond

By Mary Ann Streblow

Tickle your funny bone with cartoons by Mary Ann Streblow. Find out what Gray aliens are doing on earth, and what they think about those they encounter.

Order by phone at 1-888-232-4444, ask for it at your local bookstore, or on the internet at:
www.trafford.com/robots/03-1347.html

Book Title: Gray Folks: Earth and Beyond

Author: Mary Ann Streblow

Greetings from The MotherShip <>..<>

    I have had the privilege to have Mary Ann Streblow's Gray Folks illustrations grace the pages of my 'zines <u>The MotherShip Chronicles</u> and <u>Planet 'Zine</u>. My readers and I are delighted with her unique humorous viewpoint thru the eyes of E.T. on how they see us and handle various situations. It is like the 'Far Side' but from characters from far away. Gary Larsen had often portrayed animals in humorous situations and now we have Mary Ann Streblow portraying E.T. in their own bizarre scenarios. <u>The MotherShip Chronicles</u> is a publication that readers share their true experiences with E.T.'s and UFOS and <u>Planet 'Zine</u> is a new sci-fi, horror, fantasy publication in which Gray Folks show up as well. Both publications have been helped with Gray Folks adding the style and look that make it special. Mary is not only a talented artist, but a talented writer as well. She is also co-editor for Planet 'Zine and my biggest support base ! I wish Mary Ann and Gray Folks much success and am thankful to having been the first small press publisher to be able to feature them. Mary Ann, I am your biggest fan ! May 'Gray Folks' bring you the fame and fortune that you so well deserve !

Carol Elek , Editor-Publisher
SmartElek Publications

October 2007 Issue of the Star Beacon
Earth Star Publications
3885 Jackson Run
New Matamoras, OH 45767

Streblow's book *Gray Folks* is on the lighter side

Gray Folks: Earth and Beyond
by Mary A. Streblow
ISBN 1-412009-78-2
Trafford Publishing, Canada,
2004
122 pages, paperback.

Review by Ann Ulrich Miller

Gray Folks: Earth and Beyond is a delightful collection of Mary Streblow's clever array of cartoons with an ET theme. Mary is the cartoonist who contributed to Carol Elek's newsletter, *The MotherShip Chronicles*, now — unfortunately — out of print.

Besides being an artist, Mary Streblow has written several books, including *The Ghoulish Thoughts* series, and *Tales in the Dark*, co-authored with Sherri Kay Dobek.

The latter contains science fiction stories, supernatural, adventure and mystery.

It had to have taken a lot of imagination to come up with all the different cartoon gags in Mary's book. One common theme is that all the cartoons center around those slant-eyed Grays.

A resident of Omaha, Neb., Mary Streblow took journalism and creative writing classes in high school, and although she majored in business during college years, she became involved with the school's newspaper.

She enjoys writing short stories and in the 1980s she published a children's book, *The Knight Who Ran*.

If you like ET cartoons, you'll like this one.

Mary Streblow
© 2005

Multi-Dimensions Press
Available at Café Press

For sale are: T-shirts, totes, buttons, magnets, post cards, blank note cares and other gifts. Cat and dog designs are available. Other designs exist, such as Halloween and nature.

http://www.cafepress.com/mdpress

www.ingramcontent.com/pod-product-compliance
Lightning Source LLC
Chambersburg PA
CBHW060404030726
47497CB00003B/839